Sun

Mercury

Earth

Venus

Mars

Oxford University Press, 70 Wynford Drive, Don Mills, Ontario M3C 1J9

Toronto   Oxford   New York   Delhi   Bombay   Calcutta   Madras   Karachi
Kuala Lumpur   Singapore   Hong Kong   Tokyo   Nairobi   Dar es Salaam
Cape Town   Melbourne   Auckland   Madrid

and associated companies in
Berlin   Ibadan

Canadian Cataloguing in Publication Data
Morgan, Nicola, 1959–
Louis and the night sky

(Ox tales)
ISBN 0-19-540970-1

I. Title.   II. Series.

PS8576.0736L6 1993   jC813'.54   C92-095097-3
P27.M67Le 1993

Oxford is a trademark of Oxford University Press

1 2 3 4 — 6 5 4 3

Printed in Hong Kong

Louis
and the
Night Sky

Nicola Morgan

OXFORD UNIVERSITY PRESS
1993

*In memory of Mabel "Nanny" Lloyd
and Harold W. Tupper,
whose spirits twinkle brightly
in the night sky.*

Every night Louis was cuddled,
and then he was snuggled.
And every night, "CLICK,"
off went the light.

One night, even though
he had been cuddled and snuggled,
Louis had trouble falling asleep.
He sighed and he moaned,
and he grumbled and groaned.
But still, he couldn't sleep.

"I'm hot and thirsty," Louis mumbled.
But no one heard him.

"I'm lonely," he complained.
But still, nothing happened.
"IT'S TOO DARK IN HERE!" he called.
His parents came to his room.
"Just close your eyes, Louis," said his mother.
"Count to a hundred, Louis," said his father.

Louis tried, but he was still wide awake.

He looked out at the night sky
where the stars twinkled brightly in the dark.

Louis had an idea.

He put on his warm woolly hat
and his red winter mittens.
Then he looked out through his telescope
and found a bright star.
Louis closed his eyes tight
and made a wish.

"I want to live on a planet
where the lights are on all night long."

All of a sudden, *swishity-swoosh*,
past the moon and around the sun,
Louis was flying through the night sky.

He soared over the dry and dusty
mountains of Mercury.
Louis loved the bright colours,
but he felt hot and thirsty,
so, on he flew.

Through the night sky he soared
until he reached
the rumbling, grumbling
clouds of Venus.
"Too dark and gloomy,"
sighed Louis.
"I could never be happy here."

Louis looked into the distance
and saw something winking
far off in the night.
"That must be the place," he cried,
as he flew on to Mars,
small and red.
But when he got there,
Mars seemed tiny and alone
in the big sky.

Louis felt small and lonely too.

Louis headed towards Jupiter,
the largest of all the planets.
But there was a terrible storm raging
when he arrived.
Louis was swirled and twirled
until he felt quite dizzy and sick.

Louis sighed as he travelled on
through the night sky.
Nothing seemed right.

When he got
to the rings of Saturn,
the colours danced
before him dreamily.
"I want to dance too," he shouted
as he flew closer.

But just as he was about to step
onto one of the rings,
large chunks of rock and ice whizzed by.
Louis ducked this way and that.
In an instant he was off, still searching
for the best planet to live on.

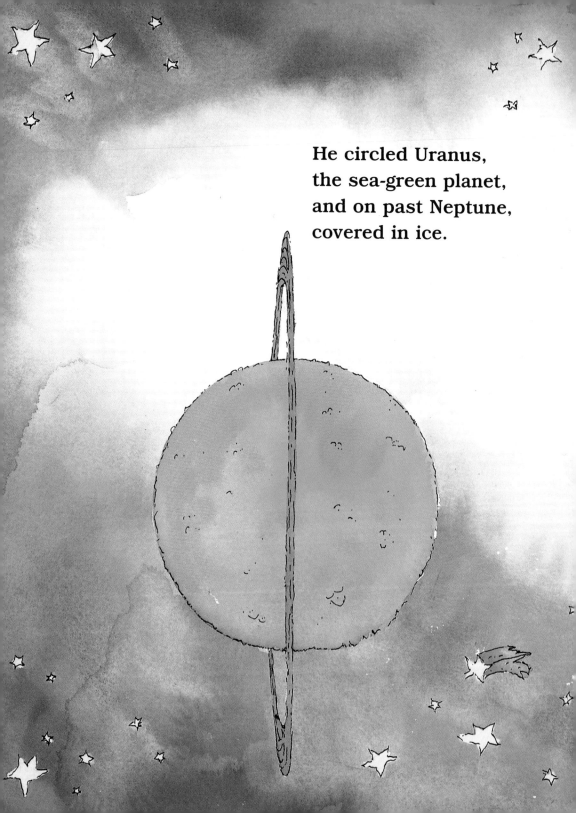

He circled Uranus,
the sea-green planet,
and on past Neptune,
covered in ice.

Louis travelled
further and further through space.
The sun's light grew faint
and the night was icy cold.
"Maybe I've gone the wrong way,"
Louis shivered. But on he flew.

When he reached Pluto,
the last planet in the night sky,
Louis could see all of space.
He had never felt so small and lonely
and cold in his whole life.
He wanted to cry,
but he was afraid that his tears would freeze.
"THERE MUST BE SOMEWHERE I CAN LIVE,"
he called.

Nobody answered.

Then Louis looked back
and saw the most wonderful sight.

Way off in the distance
a small planet twinkled
like a magic blue marble in the darkness.
It was lovelier
than any of the planets he had visited.
"How could I have missed that?" wondered Louis.

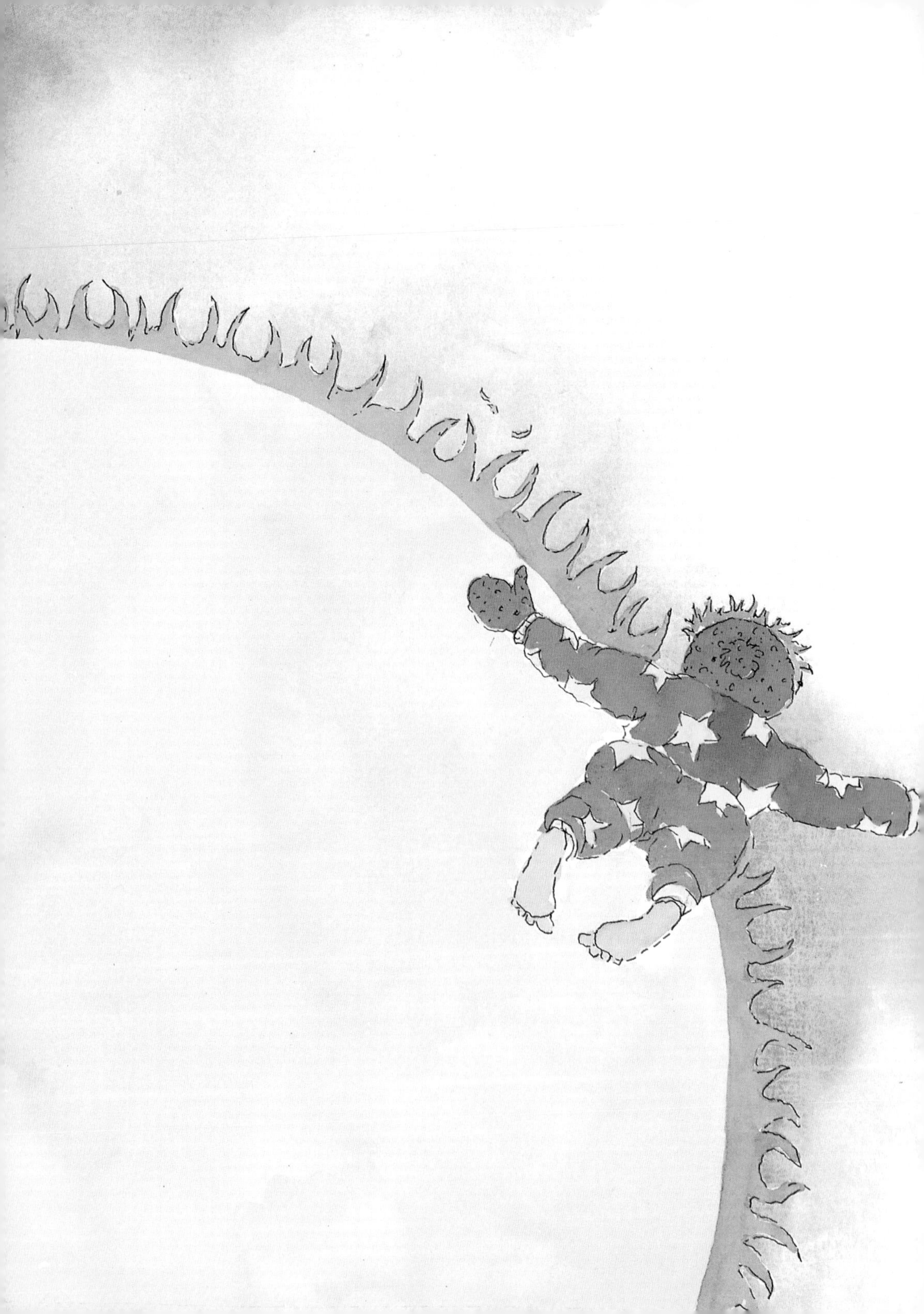

Swishity-swoosh!
Louis flew back
through the night sky
without ever taking his eyes off
the marvellous blue planet.

On and on he went, through the stars,
around the sun and past the moon.

As he got closer, Louis could see
sparkling blue oceans,
with puffy white clouds gliding gently above.
He could see trees, and snow-capped mountains
and rivers and lakes.
"It's perfect!" he shouted
as he flew even nearer.

Louis thought about his mother and father.
How they would love this beautiful planet.
Then something wonderful happened.
Louis saw his own house.

He had come home.

Louis landed
with a very loud "THUMP"
on his bedroom floor.

His parents came running to his room.
"Louis! Are you all right?" they asked.

Louis slid his warm woolly hat
and his warm winter mittens
under the bed
and with a smile he answered,
"Yes."

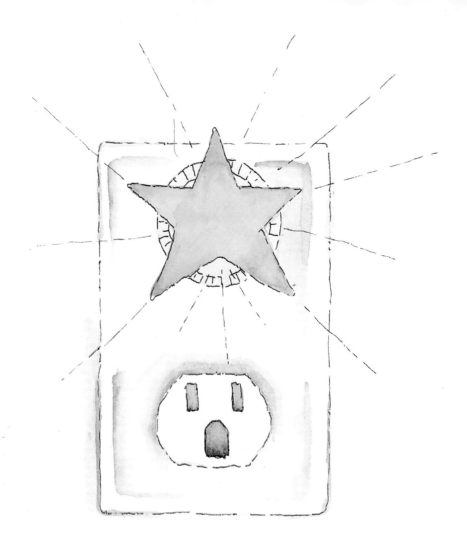

"Your room is very dark," said his mother.
"We thought this might help," said his father.

They gave Louis a small night light.
It twinkled just like a star in the sky.

Once again Louis was cuddled,
and then he was snuggled.
And "CLICK,"
off went the light.

Outside, the night sky whispered a soft goodnight.

But Louis

was already

fast

asleep.

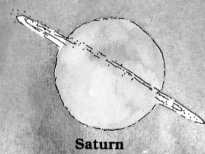

Jupiter

Saturn

Uranus

Neptune

Pluto